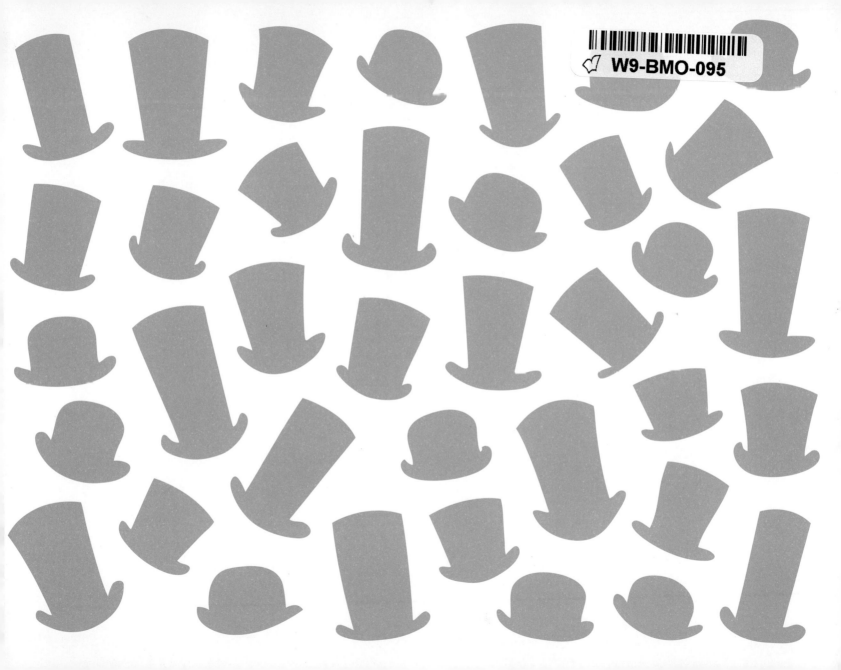

Brimsby's HATS

Andrew Prahin

Simon & Schuster Books for Young Readers

New York   London   Toronto   Sydney   New Delhi

Here's to pals.
Especially my best friend, Katie

ACKNOWLEDGMENTS

This book would not have been possible without my parents, Charles and Sheila.
Because without them, I would not exist.
Also they are magnificent, loving people who made me who I am.

I'd like to acknowledge my sisters, Jenny and Emily,
for their invaluable plumage advice.

Paul and Lori at Rodeen Literary Management; and David, Lizzy, and Navah at
Simon & Schuster are risk-takers and generous experts. This book is what it is
because I've been lucky enough to work with each of them.

Finally, I want to thank my wife, Katie, for pretty much everything.

SIMON & SCHUSTER BOOKS FOR YOUNG READERS · An imprint of Simon & Schuster Children's Publishing Division · 1230 Avenue of the Americas, New York, New York 10020 · Copyright © 2014 by Andrew Prahin · All rights reserved, including the right of reproduction in whole or in part in any form. · SIMON & SCHUSTER BOOKS FOR YOUNG READERS is a trademark of Simon & Schuster, Inc. · For information about special discounts for bulk purchases, please contact Simon & Schuster Special Sales at 1-866-506-1949 or business@simonandschuster.com. · The Simon & Schuster Speakers Bureau can bring authors to your live event. For more information or to book an event, contact the Simon & Schuster Speakers Bureau at 1-866-248-3049 or visit our website at www.simonspeakers.com. · Book design by Lizzy Bromley · The text for this book is set in La Gioconda Old Style. · The illustrations for this book are rendered in Adobe Illustrator. · Manufactured in China · 1013 SCP · 10 9 8 7 6 5 4 3 2 1 · Library of Congress Cataloging-in-Publication Data · Prahin, Andrew. · Brimsby's Hats / Andrew Prahin.—1st ed. · p. cm. · Summary: When the friend with whom he has enjoyed tea and conversation each day goes off to sea, a talented hat maker devises a creative way to make new friends. · ISBN 978-1-4424-8147-3 (hardcover : alk. paper) · ISBN 978-1-4424-8148-0 (eBook) · [1. Friendship—Fiction. 2. Hats—Fiction. 3. Creative ability—Fiction.] I. Title. · PZ7.P88646Lon 2014 · [E]—dc23 · 2012024049 ·

Once, in the quiet countryside,
a hat maker lived in a little cottage.
His best friend visited every day.

Brimsby
would make the most
wonderful hats

and his friend
would make the most
wonderful tea.

Together they would have the most wonderful conversations.

When the hats were finished,
they sent them to customers all around the world.

This was how it was for many years,

until one morning the friend said that he would be leaving to travel far away.
You see, it was his dream to become a sea captain.

The next day the hat maker gave his friend a brand-new hat. It fit perfectly.

Then he wished his friend the best of luck and waved him good-bye.

The hat maker worked for many quiet days after that, and had many quiet cups of tea.

(They weren't nearly as wonderful as the tea his friend used to make.)

Too quiet.

....................It was quiet..Very quiet.....................................

....................One day the hat maker realized he had become awfully lonely . . .

so he set out on a walk, looking to make some new friends.
He wore his favorite hat.

After traveling all day the hat maker came upon a tree full of birds.
He thought the birds would make very nice friends.

He said Hello.

But the birds didn't hear him.

They were hard at work shoveling the snow out of their nests
and keeping the cold wind from blowing out their fires.

The hat maker stood there all alone and watched
the busy birds as the snow fell and the wind blew.

Then, after it had grown dark,
he returned home through the silent snow.

He sat in his chair and looked out the window. After some time, he put his cup down.

He gathered his tools, and he took down some of his hats.

Then he went to work.

He worked all night, measuring and marking,

cutting and stitching.

When morning came the hat maker packed everything up
and carried it through the snow.

He found the tree full of busy birds, and he worked just a little bit more.

When he was finished, the birds had new homes.
The hats kept the snow out of their nests and stopped
the cold wind from blowing out their fires.

The birds weren't busy anymore.

So they all talked. They talked about hats.
They talked about snow shovels. They talked about
whether lemon cookies taste better than worms.

And when it got late, the hat maker said good-bye to his new friends and walked home.

That night the birds
went to bed in warm houses,
and they were very happy.

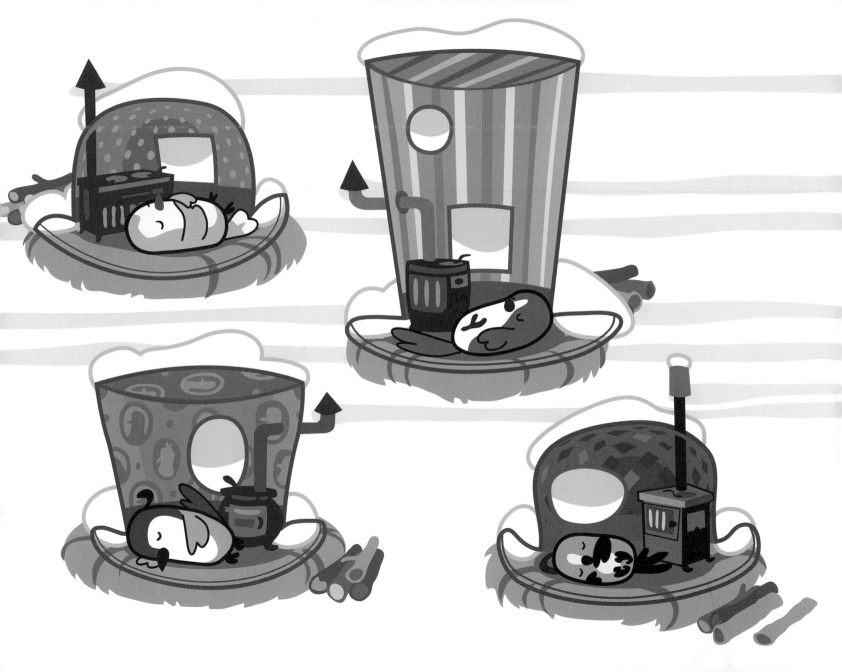

They weren't the only ones.

From then on, the hat maker
and the birds would see
one another quite often.
Sometimes the hat maker
would visit the birds.

And sometimes
the birds would visit
the hat maker.

But every once in a while,
they would all take a very long journey.

They would travel to a seaside town that was full of ships, to visit an old friend.

And the large group of friends would drink tea and talk about hats and shovels and ships and how wonderful it was that they had all been lucky enough to meet one another.

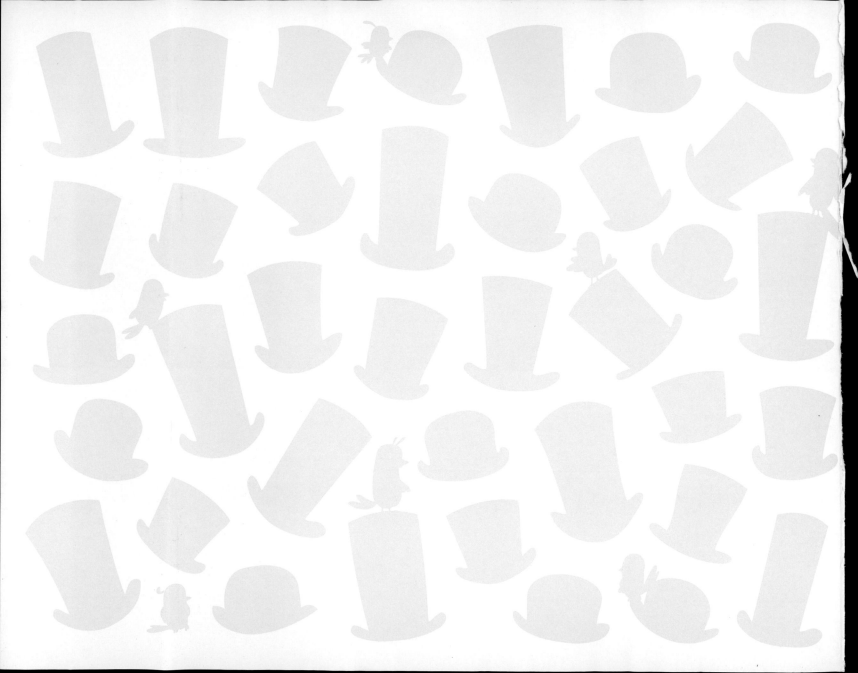